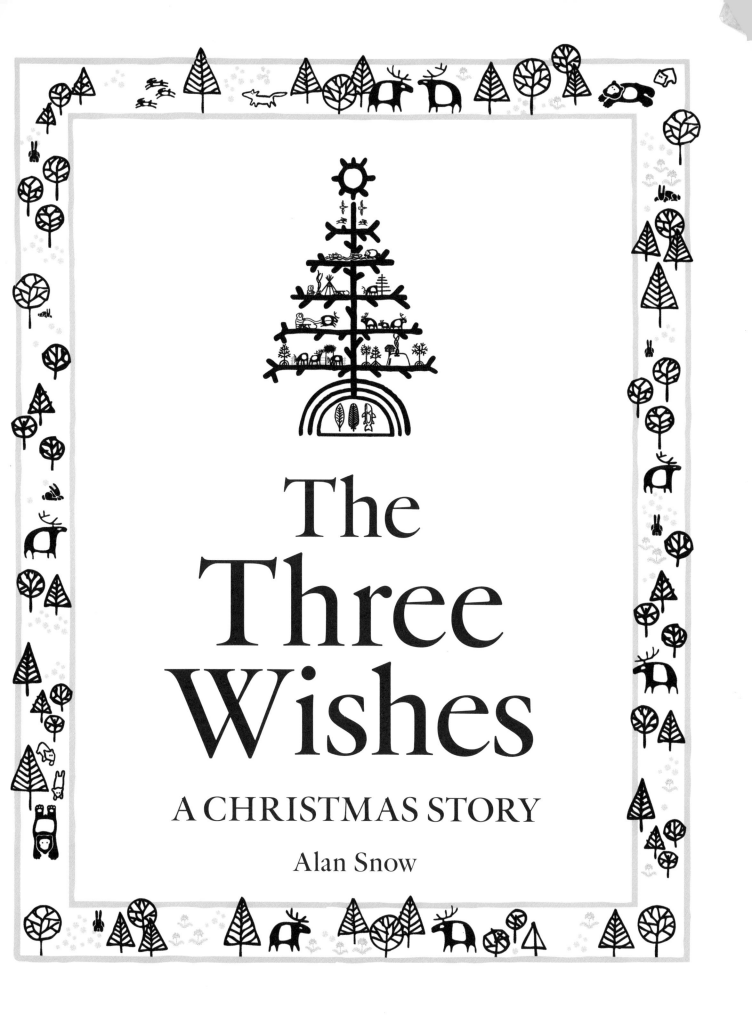

The Three Wishes

A CHRISTMAS STORY

Alan Snow

Long, long ago in the very north a group of people lived with the reindeer. In summer they would move as family groups, sleeping in tents and travelling on sledges drawn by their deer. The adults would hunt and forage, while the children would look after the deer, and play.

When autumn came, the families would head south for the great annual gathering of their people. As they travelled they would round up any deer they found along the way.

When the families arrived at the meeting ground the deer would be herded into a corral, and then it would be time for feasting. Everyone would help to prepare the great meal and once they had all eaten there would be

the telling of tales, the exchange of news, and some years even a wedding.
Then, as it grew dark, the children would play with their old friends
and join in the singing of songs.

When the gathering was over the families would divide again and travel to the forests. Here, each family would find one of the winter lodges that had been built over the years and prepare for the dark months, cutting and storing feed for the deer, collecting nuts and berries, and making sure their lodge was ready for the snows.

When the days grew shorter and the snows arrived the families would retire to their lodges. Here they would make new clothes and tools, tell tales, and settle in for the time of darkness.

In one particular family it fell to the elder child to feed the deer. As the days grew shorter, the boy, who was afraid of the dark, would rush his tasks so he could return to the warmth and safety of the lodge.

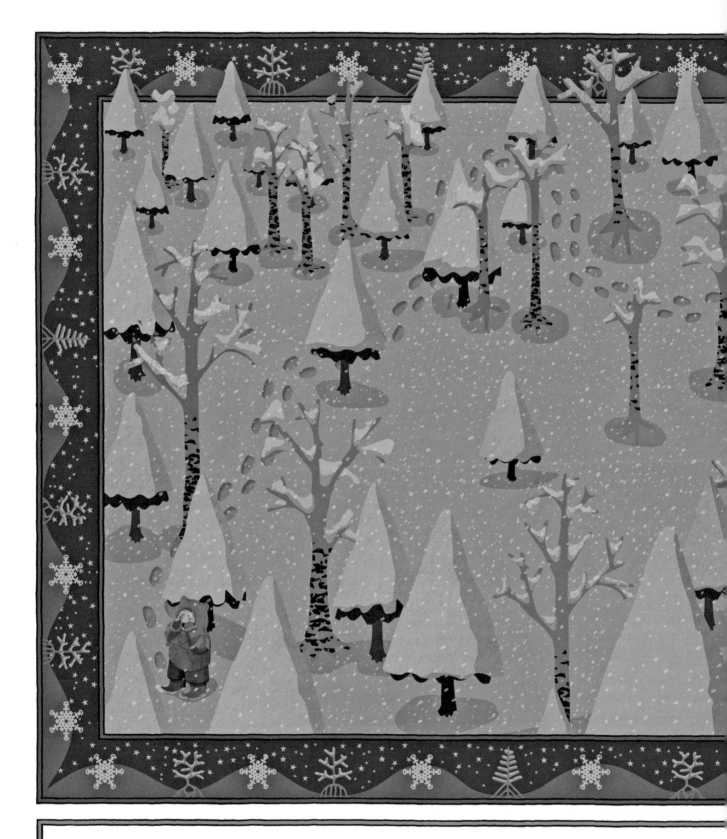

It came to the very darkest time when the sun did not rise at all. The boy left the lodge and approached the corral, but saw that the gate was already open. He ran to see if the deer were still there. They were not. What was he to do? The family could not survive without their animals.

The boy ran out into the forest, calling to the deer.

He stopped to listen, but all was silent. The snow now started to fall heavily. He ran further into the forest. Within a few minutes he was lost.

The boy started to shiver and soon his strength seeped away. Tiredness swept over him and slowly he sank to the ground.

He lay on the snow and his eyes grew very heavy. Just as he was about to give in to sleep, there came the sound of a reindeer bell.

The boy's eyes opened. He heard the sound again. Raising himself from the snow, he started to move in the direction of the bell.

As he walked through the trees the sound grew louder and at last he could see the reindeer. They were gathered around the entrance to a cave.

Just inside the cave stood a small creature, seemingly made of wood. It was taking handfuls of fresh grass from a large bag and feeding the deer.

Suddenly the deer followed the wood creature into the cave, which tilted down into the ground. The boy chased as fast as he could, but the deer kept ahead of him.

After a while the cave changed about him. The ground became soft, the roof became leaves and the walls turned from stone to bark.

Light came flooding in. The boy looked about him and saw that he was inside a vast cave, so large that it held its own sun. All was warm and green.

Three small creatures approached him. The first was the being who seemed to be made from wood. The second was part fish, and the last was bird-like.

"What are you doing here?" asked the wood creature.
"I was chasing my deer. What is this place?" said the boy.
"This is the home of summer and we tend it," answered the fish.
"It is beautiful... but I must take my deer and go back to the outer world,"
said the boy.

"That, I am sorry to say, is not possible," the bird declared.

"The summer must protect itself, for it needs to rest here undisturbed.
Those in the outer world must not know of this place.

"If you return, time will stop and you may never tell," said the wood creature.

"Then what am I to do?" cried the boy.

"You may stay with us and help us… and in return we will grant you three wishes," said the bird.

The boy thought for a moment and then spoke. "It is very easy. For my first wish I want freedom. And for my second, happiness!"

"Those you may have, but only with time," replied the wood creature.

The boy thought deeply and finally spoke again. "Then there is only one thing more that I wish for, and that is time."

"You will be granted time," replied the fish. "You may not know it but you have chosen well."

It never grew dark. The boy forgot some of his sadness as he learned about nature and helped to tend the trees and plants.

In the time of spring the bird flew into the sky,
drawing some of the summer into the outer world.

In the autumn it returned on the wind.

At the end of the year, the creatures held a feast.

"You have done well, boy," they said to him. "You must be rewarded."

"Please, I need to know that my family are well!"

The friends looked at each other and the wood creature spoke.

"At this time when it is darkest in the outer world, I think you might return to check upon them. But you must return here or their lives will not continue. Tonight you may visit your family."

The boy rushed to put on his winter clothes, then ran to the tunnel
and up into the outer world. The moment he stepped out of the cave
the snow that was falling froze in the air.

He made his way back to the lodge his family had used last year, and climbed in through the chimney.

Before him, asleep, lay his uncle and aunt. The boy clambered out and ran into the forest to find the next lodge. If his uncle and aunt were in this first lodge, his other family would be close by. He found the next lodge and climbed inside.

His parents lay asleep. All was still. The fire flames did not move, the smoke was frozen in the air. The boy went to his parents and tried to wake them, but could not. He then turned to his sister's bed and tried to wake her. Again, he could not.

He took from his pocket a carved deer that his mother had made for him many years earlier. He placed it by his sister's pillow as a sign that he had returned. He kissed his sister, then his parents and left the lodge to return to the cave.

During his second year in the cave the boy worked with the fish, helping to tend the streams and pools, and all of the creatures that lived in them.

There was much work to do and the boy helped with clearing the streams so the water could flow freely across the land. The boy learnt to swim well and the fish, pleased with him, showed him where to find pearls and how to gather them.

By the end of the year the boy had collected a great number
of pearls. He asked if he could return again to visit his parents
and leave them as a gift. The creatures agreed and, when it was
darkest in the outside world, the boy departed.

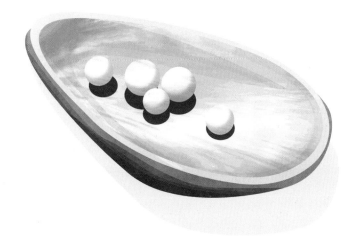

As he left the cave the snow again became still in the air. The boy visited several lodges before he found his family. He placed the pearls in shells by their beds, watched over them for a while, kissed them goodbye and returned to the cave.

In the third year the boy helped the bird. He learned of the creatures of the air, how the winds carried the seasons, brought water in the rain to refresh the land, and how insects carried pollen from flower to flower.

At the end of that year the bird spoke.

"Boy, you show much kindness and it is clear that your love for your family is great. I shall give you four of my feathers. Take them with you when you travel to the outer world and they will speed your journey."

Then the friends gave the boy another gift. A sleigh that they had built in secret.

Upon the sleigh they placed a sack of apples and some pearls for him to take to the outer world.

The bird tied the feathers to the deer's harness.

When the boy called to the deer to set off he was startled as the sleigh rose into the air. The feathers held magic.

He travelled swiftly through the air and, after searching many lodges and leaving small gifts at each one, he found his parents.

This time, when he entered his family's lodge, something was different.
His family had recognized the pattern of his returns, and there in front of the fire
was a meal laid out for him and a new set of clothes.

The boy felt great joy, and sat by his family as he ate the food.
He put on the new clothes, which fitted him perfectly.
Then he returned to the cave.

Each year he returned to the outer world. And each year he travelled further, leaving gifts as signs of his return and his love for all.

In doing so he found freedom and happiness.
And above all, he had these things for all time.

For Izzy, Cheri, Finn, Mary, George,
Ally, Sophie, Betsy, Annie-May,
Marian, Errol, Alice and Poppy

First published in the United Kingdom in 2020 by
Pavilion Children's Books
43 Great Ormond Street
London
WC1N 3HZ

An imprint of Pavilion Books Company Limited.

Publisher: Neil Dunnicliffe
Editor: Hattie Grylls

ISBN: 9781843653868

A CIP catalogue record for this book is available from the British Library.

10 9 8 7 6 5 4 3 2 1

Reproduction by Rival Colour Ltd
Printed by Leo Paper Products Ltd., China

This book can be ordered directly from the publisher online at www.pavilionbooks.com,
or try your local bookshop.